FLOOD

Alvaro F. Villa

Picture Window Books

capstonepub.com

FLOOD is published by
Picture Window Books
a Capstone imprint
1710 Roe Crest Drive
North Mankato, Minnesota 56003
www.capstonepub.com

Library of Congress Cataloging-in-Publication data is
available on the Library of Congress website.

ISBN: 978-1-4048-8006-1

Designer: Russell John Griesmer

Printed in China.
092012
006934LEOS13